I hope Jo is home.
She will play with me.

Jo will pet my coat.
She will pat my nose.
Jo will give me a bone.

I will dig a hole.
I will hide the bone.
I will put it by the pole.

Jo and I will roll down the hill.
We will roll and roll.

Jo will load her bike.
She and I may go down the road.
I will run.

Jo will get a cone for us.
I will like the cone.

We may roam to the cove.
We will look at boats.
It will be fun.

Is Jo home?
No, not yet.
I will doze and wait.